Asma Almansoori is not fond of reading books, why is that? Because she finds them boring and they do not have pictures. Unlike her, people use their imagination while reading. She wrote this book trying to change her point of view on books. While doing that, she was finally able to find her lost imagination. That is how *The Half Child* was created.

To my 16 years old self.

I did it.

Asma Almansoori

THE HALF CHILD

AUSTIN MACAULEY PUBLISHERS™

LONDON • CAMBRIDGE • NEW YORK • SHARJAH

ISBN – 9789948817383 – (Paperback)
ISBN – 9789948817390 – (E-Book)

Application Number: MC-10-01-8388781
Age Classification: 13+

First Published 2022
AUSTIN MACAULEY PUBLISHERS FZE
Sharjah Publishing City
P.O Box [519201]
Sharjah, UAE
www.austinmacauley.ae
+971 655 95 202

I just want to thank Austin Macauley Publishers for their hard work. I wouldn't be able to do it without you.

The Tragedy in the Forest

Everyone in this world has something different from the other, some about their looks, others about their personality. However, I am completely different. I have red eyes and red hair, I have powers…and that is it, nothing special. Anyway, I live in a world where demons, vampires and humans live together, even though they hate each other. STRANGE, right!? There is a reason why they live peacefully together, but this story is not about that. This story is about what happened after the three worlds became one.

It all started when I was first born, my parents named me Licht. My family was quite rich. We lived in the middle of the forest, outside the forest there was a small village and the humans lived there. For some reason, the humans called the forest, "the demon's forest." At that time, I did not know anything about it because I was too young. I was 7 years old. I lived a normal life with my parents and the strange mysterious creatures. I woke up every morning, showered, ate my breakfast and went outside. Every day those mysterious creatures came and played with me. Even though I knew they were not humans or animals and they looked somewhat scary, I did not care, since they always played with me and treated me nicely. Every day was the same and every day I met a new creature. I could play anytime I wanted, but I had to go home at 8 o'clock at night, they say dangerous creatures comes after that.

After two years, everything in my life changed. It was midnight, I heard a crashing sound. I walked toward the sound; it became louder. When I stopped, it was my mom and dad's room. I opened the door slowly to see a room filled with blood, I saw my parents on the floor. I was shocked by this scene, I tried to run but my body felt as heavy as lead. At that moment, a man suddenly appeared behind me, I slowly turned my head to see him. He was tall, had red eyes and sharp fangs. He looked exactly like humans, but that was impossible because humans do not have red eyes. I thought he was a vampire. That man kept staring at me. I was trembling, my tears rolled down to my cheek, but then he walked to the window and ran away. My heart was beating so fast, I collapsed where I was standing.

Everything was black, I heard my mother's voice calling me, but her voice suddenly disappeared. I opened my eyes and I was in a room. I saw an old man standing beside the window, he was looking at me with his scary eyes.

The Strange Old Man

When I woke up, I saw an old man staring at me with his scary eyes. The old man was tall, his form was similar to humans and he had a long white beard, he also had a cane in his hand. He walked toward the bed and asked, "Are you okay?"

"I'm okay," I replied. Then he went outside the room without saying anything. That felt strange for a while, but then I suddenly got dizzy and lost consciousness. Again, darkness was surrounding me, could not see anything. However, pieces of small golden light appeared from nowhere. They were everywhere, I tried to hold one of them, but the light became brighter. I closed my eyes and when I opened them, I saw my house in front of me. I looked around me, I saw my parents standing there. When I tried to approach them, they got farther away and disappeared. Was it my hallucination, or did the accident affect my brain into imagining strange things?

I opened my eyes and the room was dark. It was night. I got off the bed and the old man entered the room. "You finally woke up, these are new clothes for you. Wear them and follow me," said the old man. I put the clothes on quickly and followed him. He took me to a larger room, there was a long table and lots of chairs there. Well, everything seems to be big for a small kid but whatever. He told me to sit, and as soon he clapped his hand, the butler came with lots of food. "Eat what you want, when you're finished, the demons will escort you to my room. I will be waiting," he said.

"Wait, what demons?" I said. Then he pointed at the roof, I looked up and saw lots of red eyes looking at me. It is scary when you see it, as if you are in a haunted house or something. They all fell behind the old man and they were shorter than me.

"These creatures are demons, maybe you don't know them, but you have already seen creatures similar to them," he said. I nodded my head and the old man left the room.

I started eating, it felt awkward because the demons kept staring at me as if they were going to attack me or something. When I finished, a small demon held my hand and walked me to the old man's room. I knocked on the door and entered the room. "Oh, you are finally here, come sit on the chair. I have something to tell you," he said. I went inside and closed the door. "I assume that you have a lot of questions right now, but don't worry, I will tell you what you need to know for now," he said.

"As for me, my name is John Sandford and I am your father's best friend. When he sensed that danger was approaching you and your mother, he sent me a letter saying that I should take you with me if something happened to them."

As he continued, I was silently listening to him.

The Discovery of Secrets

John, the old man, kept talking about strange things that I couldn't understand. I interrupted him and said, "Sorry, but it's hard for me to understand all this, so give me some time to realize what you are saying."

He looked at me with his scary eyes and said, "Fine, it is dark anyway so go rest and I will continue tomorrow." He clapped his hands again and the little demon opened the door and John told him to escort me to my room. The little demon took my hand and we went together.

Next day when I woke up, I saw a lot of demons gathered around the bed. They were staring at me and it felt awkward. John entered the room and the demons rushed to him, they bowed down and greeted him. That felt strange for a moment, but I thought maybe because they are his servants, or maybe they are scared because that old man looks scary. After breakfast, John and I went upstairs, we walked through the long hallway. It wasn't long, but I was tired. He stopped in front a door and told me to open it. When I did, I saw a lot of pictures. There was also a picture of my parents. "What is this room?" I asked, he told me that this room is for the pictures of the kings that rule the demon and vampire worlds. One side was for the demons' world kings and the other was for the vampires' world kings, and my parents' picture was in the center.

"But what does it have to do with me?" I said.

"I'm showing this to you because someday your picture will be hanging here, you are the next king who will rule both worlds, the demons' and the vampires'. It will take time to explain everything, so I will just tell you about your family, and the tragedy that happened that night," he said. Then he brought two chairs and told me to sit because it might take a long time.

"I want you to listen carefully so you can understand what I say." I nodded my head and opened my ears, at last all the secrets would be discovered. Well, not all of them but who cares.

"First of all, let me tell you this. There are three worlds, first the human world and you already know it. The second is the demon world where all kinds of demons live, only strong demons can take any form they want to hide their true self. However, when demons change their form, they become less powerful. Last is the vampire world, vampires also look like humans, but they have red eyes, long nails that cut like swords, sharp fangs, bat wings and some vampires with pure blood can turn themselves into bats. Vampires with pure blood means that they were born as a vampire and both of their parents are vampires. The reason why pure blood vampires are special is because most vampires were originally humans turned into vampires, so they are not as strong as the pure blood vampires. However, it's different with demons. It's rare to see demons who were originally humans. Demons always thought that they were above both humans and vampires, that's why humans turning into demons are rare cases. It's still rare till this day."

He said three worlds, but it's actually one world. He meant to say the world was divided into three territories which are demons, vampires and humans.

"Your mother, Maria, was a pure blood vampire princess. Your father, Vincent, was the king of the demons. Which makes you a half demon and half vampire. They married each other and you were born. They wanted to keep you safe, that's why they chose the forest to live in, away from danger. What happened that night was terrible. Before midnight, your father sensed an evil aura coming closer to your house, so he sent me a message asking for help, but when I arrived, it was too late. Both of your parents were dead, and when I saw you, I thought you were dead at first. There was no blood around you, so I checked your pulse. I was relieved to know that you were still alive, so I took you with me and ran away in case if someone was still there.

"As for this house, it's mine but you can live here as long as you want to. This is all I can tell you right now, don't worry you have so much time to know about other things." That was the last thing John told me before he left. I stayed in the room, staring at my parent's picture. All that happened was to protect me, I wanted to become stronger so I could avenge my parent's death. That's what I thought about. I rushed to John to ask him to teach me how to become stronger. I was not sure what he will say, but at least I wanted to ask him.

I continued running after John, but he walked too fast. Then, I remembered what John said, he said that my father was a demon, so why did he look like humans. As I ran, I shouted his name, he stopped and I bumped into him. "What are you doing chasing after me?" he said.

I stood up and said, "I want to ask you something. You said that my father was a demon, but he looked like a human. Please explain that to me, I'm confused."

"I have already told, didn't I," he said. "Okay listen well, your father was a demon. I told you that strong demons can change their forms into anything they want. He didn't want you to see him in his scary demon form, so he changed his form for you."

"Umm, so now it's clear, can I ask for a favor. I want you to train me so I can become stronger, it's okay if you don't want to." I said that but then he suddenly started laughing, did I said something funny, or maybe he didn't take me seriously…

Decision

Maybe there's something wrong with him but he's laughing too hard. Is it too funny to ask him to train me, or is he looking down on me? "Hey," I shouted, "what's wrong with you, did I say something funny?"

"Sorry about that," he said. "But for a brat like you to learn how to fight, I find it way too funny." After that he left with the biggest smile on his face, and at the same time, I became furious with what had happened, so I returned to my room.

I wanted to hit him, but with my shortness I was not sure how to do it.

I slammed the door so hard, even the little demons in my room ran away. I knew why he laughed at me, since those words came from a nine-year-old boy. It is natural to laugh because it sounds ridiculous. *I think there's still time before lunch,* I thought. I went for a walk inside John's house.

On my way I saw John talking with a demon, I wanted to ignore him but as soon as he saw me, he said, "Did the crybaby finished crying over his hopeless dream?" and put the biggest smile on his face.

"Shut up," I said, then I walked away. I got really angry, but as they say, if you want to do something, don't rely on others, well I say that. If I want to become stronger then I must rely on myself, the problem was that I didn't know where to start or what to do.

I thought about a lot of things while I was walking and because of that, I lost my way. I didn't know where I was. There were lots of doors and no one was there. I panicked, then the little demon appeared behind me. "The lunch is ready young master," he said. He held my hand and took me to the dining room. John was there eating, we entered the room and he glared at me.

"If you want to walk around the house then tell me, how would I know if you were safe or not," he said. "Anyway eat your lunch, you must be starving." I apologized to him and started eating, even though I didn't want to apologize. He didn't even wait for me to come, he just started eating while knowing I was lost.

When we finished, he told me about a school that is only for vampires and demons. "What do you think of it? I won't be able to teach you everything but if you went to that school, you will learn more than making me teach you," he said.

Since he mentioned the school, maybe he never wanted to teach me, or did he know what was best for me. Again, going to school might be better. If he was my teacher, he would make fun of me every day, so I thought that going to school was better. I decided to go to the school, and I told him that I will go. "Very well, in two weeks you will be attending the best school ever, so be ready," he said. Again, he put the biggest smile on his face, for some reason I sensed a dark aura coming out of that old man. After all, going to school might not be bad because I will meet lots of different creatures. I was so excited and couldn't wait till my first day of school.

John did all the paperwork and prepared my luggage for me. The butler took the luggage to the cart and was waiting for me. "The school offer bedrooms for the students, so you will be staying there for a long time," he said. That means I will not see him for years. That was good news for me, but I didn't tell him because he will hit me. "You will not see me in a long time, so I have three rules for you," he said. "First, do not mention me to anyone. If they asked about your guardian, tell them that I am your uncle. Second, don't tell anyone that you are a prince. From now on, you will be a normal kid who lives with his uncle. Everyone think that you are dead. Finally, don't trust anyone easily." With these rules, I am sure I can live a peaceful life, but the problem is my appearance. I told him about it, but he said it will be okay because no one knows what the prince, me, looks like. After that, I left his house heading to the school.

School Life

My journey to the school was too boring, trees were the only thing out there. It took hours, but I was finally there. There were five people waiting outside the school, three boys and two girls. They looked similar, all of them had black hair and red eyes. "Hello and welcome to our school, we are happy to have you here. I'm the president of the student council, my name is Allen. Nice to meet you," he said. "Your luggage will be taken to your room. I will show you around the school first and you will start your first day of school tomorrow."

We went inside, and there was a huge picture in the middle and stairs on both sides. Allen told me that the picture was for the person who established the school. He said the stairs on the right side took you to your classes, the stairs on the left side are for the teachers and the student council. He first showed me the meeting room where the student council helped the students, then he showed me the classes. "I've heard from your uncle that you are half demon and half vampire. It's rare to see someone like you, but I'm sure you will get along with the rest of the students. There are some mixed students like you, but you can count them on fingers. Mixed children are still rare to see after all. Don't worry, there is no discrimination in this school," he said.

Allen said since I was mixed, I must learn about both sides. Allen then asked one of the student council members to continue the tour before leaving with the rest of the members to attend other students. "Licht, it's nice to meet you. I'm part of the student council, my name is Lilly," she said. "For your subjects, you will be taking history and P.E. For P.E. classes, you will be learning how to use and control your powers. It might be difficult for you because you are a mix, but I'm sure you will be able to do it." She showed me the classes and the library. The library was huge, and it had lots of books. After that, she took me to the students' dorm where I would be staying. She said that students must not share their rooms to other, it's a rule. She left so I can prepare myself for tomorrow, but I was so tired, so I just went to sleep.

Next day, they gathered all the students outside. There were 100 students including myself. It was weird to know that only 100 students attended the school. John said that it was the best school, but the number of students was so low, that made the school looks suspicious. After that, they divided us into five classes, each class had 20 students in it. Then our homeroom teachers took us to the class and we just introduced ourselves to each other.

The Kidnapping

Nothing interesting happened during my time in school, we spent our life in school normally. Years has passed, and we became closer with each other. Everything was going so well, except for one thing that made the students run away from the school.

After eight years of attending the school, there were only fifty students in the school. We discovered that during these years, fifty students had gone missing. We asked our teacher and the student council, but all they said was, "Don't worry, everything is under control. The missing students are just uniting with their families." The number of missing students was increasing, and the students were going crazy. They started to think that there was a kidnapper among the students or the teachers, but no one did anything. It may sound ridiculous hearing that students were being kidnapped, and I agree to that. People at this age love to make everything into a drama or mystery. Skipping classes might have been a possible reason, but they already think it's kidnapping which made convincing them harder. They also ignored the fact that the teachers said the missing students are just being with their families.

One night, I woke up hearing someone scream. I wanted to go and check, but once I opened the door, I found Allen standing outside. I told him about the screams, but he said it's okay and closed the door. I tried to open it again, but I couldn't do it because it was locked. I couldn't sleep either, so I just stayed in my room until it's time for school. In the morning, I went to class and everyone was talking about what happened last night. No one went to check because they were too scared. Some of them said the student council members prevented them from going outside of their rooms by locking the doors.

After they stopped talking, one of them suggested that we should put an end to what's happening. They chose five students to fake their sleep and hide somewhere in the dorm, of course I was one of them. Maybe you're thinking why I am doing this with them, well the reason for that is because I was forced to. It also sounds fun spying on others, but don't do it. Honestly, I didn't think it will happen again, but I helped them anyway.

The night came, and we heard it again. I saw two persons holding one of the students and taking him to the school, the five of us went after them without them noticing. It was strange that the student council wasn't there to stop us, but thanks to that we continued to follow them without any problem. They took him to the teacher's side of the school and went inside a huge black door. We waited for a while and slowly opened the door, what was inside surprised us all. The students who were supposed to be missing, we found them inside. We later discovered that the kidnappers are the teachers themselves. They were torturing the students to death; their bodies were kept inside for no reason.

The scene was horrifying, we couldn't move a muscle. After a while, we returned to the dorm and all of them just went to their rooms without saying anything.

Next morning, we stood in front of the dorm's door without letting anyone leave. We told them what we saw and decided to run away. We left everything behind and escaped to forest, but later we found our teachers chasing after us. We ran as fast as we can, but so many were killed. Luckily for me, a stranger came out of nowhere and helped me escape. He took me to an old house beside a river and told me to stay there, then he left.

History

After hours of waiting, the stranger returned to where I was. He opened the door and told me that it's safe now, he also told me that John is waiting for me. A cart was waiting outside, and John's butler was standing there. The butler said that we should escape from here because it's still dangerous for me. My journey to John's house was again boring, but we arrived before night. I entered the house and the little demon took me to John's room. John was so thrilled to see me, but I wasn't. "Look at you, look at how mature you became after going to school. You should be thanking me," he said. As always, he didn't know how to compliment someone.

I spent the night telling him about the school and the kidnappers. "You know, it's not the first time for something like this to happen. Kids in your age or younger are found dead in different places, including schools. I have sent one of my servants to look after you just in case if something happens to you, but I never expected something like this to happen to you," he said. I was shocked to know that he worried about me, maybe he really cares about me. Then he changed the subject and asked me whether I learnt something or not, especially the history behind the three worlds becoming one. I couldn't tell him that I was sleeping during history class, so I tried to make something up. "An idiot will always be an idiot no matter what. How do you plan to become the next king without knowing anything about your ancestors?" he said. Then I got punched by him. I will correct what I said before, this old man will never care about anyone ever. He has no mercy on anyone.

If he knew that kids at my age are being killed, why did he send me to that school. He also appointed someone to watch me from afar, does he seriously want me to be killed or am I thinking too much.

I was forced to listen to him talking about our ancestors all night. "Listen well, before uniting the three worlds, everyone lived in fear. The weak ones died, and the strong ones survived by using others. That's how everyone lived their lives, until a noble vampire fell in love with a human princess and decided to marry her. None of the demons, vampires or humans agreed to their marriage, but then a council was formed. The council had five noble demons, five noble vampires and five noble humans, it was formed to bring peace between them all. It didn't work at first, but peace was obtained when one of the five noble demons decided to marry another noble vampire and rule over the world. Everything was fine until the recent tragedy that happened to your parent. After they died, kids are found dead, especially mixed kids like you. They didn't stop there, when they couldn't find mixed children, they went after demons' and vampires' children," he said. As he continued, I was already half asleep.

I won't tell him that I was sleeping instead of listening to him, sleeping with your eyes open is a technique I learnt back in school. If I told him, I would be dead by now.

Identity?

It has been a week since I went outside, John wouldn't let me because it's too dangerous. I tried to convince him, but he won't listen to me. He said that they will come after me if I went outside for a second. I was mad at him, why is it okay for him to go outside and not for me. I asked the little demon to show me the rest of the house since it's a huge house. Nothing was interesting, just empty rooms.

I came up with a plan that would allow me to go outside, I will keep annoying him until he gives up. After two weeks, he finally agreed. It took time, but I succeeded at the end. During these two weeks, I learned to be patient in order to get what I want. The only problem is that I must take the butler with me, he won't trust me no matter what. I finally went outside with the butler; we were just walking around the area at night. Without realizing, I went far away from the house. The butler was following me from behind and he didn't say anything. The moment I opened my mouth, a group of vampires attacked us.

Of course, I was able to defeat them all except for one who was hiding behind the trees. I was able to catch him before he ran away. I wanted to get some information from him, so I started asking him some questions. He refused to talk, so I scared him a little. He glared at me and said, "It's not our fault, it's all his fault. Leaving a pregnant woman behind without a reason, faking his love to her. We are only victims of her madness. You have to know that you are in a great danger." That were his last words before being killed by the butler. I just noticed that I was battling the bad guys while the butler was standing there watching me.

"I could have used some help you know," I said.

"I know you're strong, so there is no need for me to help you," the butler replied. Honestly, does no one cares if I die or not. Well, the bad guys were knocked down by just kicking and punching them. Does that count as being strong, or are they just weak?

After that, the butler silently showed me the way to John's house. We went back and told the old man everything, it was my first time seeing him frightened. If this fearless old man got scared after hearing that, then we are indeed in a great danger. I say that, but I don't know why I held my laughter after seeing him scared. I mean, getting scared does not suit him at all. I would have gotten away with holding my laughter if it wasn't for the butler telling John about it. Because of that I got punched again. For an old man, his punches hurt a lot.

John was panicking, the butler was trying so hard to calm him down. He then gave an order to the butler to gather all the demons in the house in the meeting room. He turned to me and said, "You should go to your room and rest, there is nothing else for you to do here." After he left, I stood there like an idiot being left out. I had so many questions unanswered but seeing all the ruckus happening in the house, it's better to just leave things as it is for now and go rest.

Next morning, I was left eating breakfast alone. No one was there except for the butler. I asked him about John's condition, but he just replied with, "He's busy right now." The door suddenly opened, John walked in slowly with his crane in one hand and a butler holding his other hand helping him walk properly. Dark circles under his eyes, and he's barely walking straight.

"You look terrible, are you okay?" I said.

"Worry about yourself. I was up all night trying to come up with some type of protection that will keep the enemies away. We will be okay for few months without any disruption from the bad guys," John replied with an exhausted look on his face.

He sat down and asked the butler for a cup of coffee.

"So, who are we fighting against?" I said.

"Didn't you hear it from the guy you caught, that lunatic woman has completely lost her mind. If we are not careful enough, we might end up dead," he said.

I felt like he knew who she was, but purposely kept quiet about it. I didn't want to shower him with questions seeing the state he's in. For now, I know that she's powerful enough to control people surrounding her. According to that guy, her husband made her pregnant then left her. Was he playing with her? That guy said that her husband didn't love her, that's why he left her when she was pregnant. If that's so, what about those innocent children who were killed and tortured by her command. Why did she do that in the first place. Getting dumbed by someone she loved does not justify her actions. That doesn't make any sense. There's more to the story that need to be uncovered. I felt like my head is going to explode with all these questions unanswered.

"John, I know this is not a good time, but I have a lot of questions about this situation," I said.

"Well, it's normal for you to question everything giving what's happening right now. You have to excuse me for today. I have other things to do. I will answer your questions tomorrow," said John before leaving the room.

Did he just run away to avoid talking about the situation? No, I must be thinking too hard. He must be tired, that's why he left.

It was still morning, there was no one in the house except for John and his butlers. All the demons were gone. All his butlers were busy taking care of his house. I was left wandering around the house all alone. I went to check other rooms, but they were all empty.

"There's a library in this house if you wish to read to pass time," said the butler following me.

"Don't just pop out of nowhere, you scared me," I said.

"My apologies. Master John has ordered me to follow you around to prevent you from doing anything stupid. His words not mine," said the butler.

"It must be fun for you, huh. By the way, I still don't know your name. Tell me your name if you are going to follow me anywhere from now on," I said.

"My name is Alfred, young master. From now on, I will be at your service," said Alfred the butler.

After that he took me to the library. It was spacious. I didn't like to read that much but it was a way of passing time. No one's here anyway, so there's no harm in checking few books.

Preparations

Next morning came, I headed down for breakfast. I entered the dining room and saw John sitting at the table eating. As always, he never waits for me to come. Seems like food is more important to him than anything else.

"You could have waited for me to come, isn't it rude to start eating without me," I said.

"The food will be cold once you arrive. You started eating before my arrival yesterday. So, what's the difference?" John said.

Hearing what he said, he seemed better than ever. I didn't expect this childish behavior from him, new day new john.

After finishing breakfast, John, Alfred and I went to the library. For some reason, he seemed surprised when I told him that I already visited the library before. Like, I can read you know, but it's not like I enjoyed it. Also, it was Alfred's idea to go to the library not mine. Honestly, I would be surprised too if it was my decision to visit the library.

"Since you have been here before, I assume you've read some books. Anything caught your attention?," John said.

"Nothing. Books are boring. If they don't have pictures, I wouldn't bother with them," I said.

"Some people use their imagination, young master," said Alfred with a tone of mockery.

"I bet he doesn't have one," John said while giggling.

"Why are you two teaming up against me? Must be fun to tease others," I said.

Later, John told Alfred to go outside to check on the demons he sent somewhere. He must have sent all the demons outside of the house for protection. He also wanted to have some private conversation with me. He started off by asking me about the power control/training that we did back in school. Back then, we were given a P.E. class in order to know how to use and control our powers. However, that wasn't the case. All we did in P.E. class was some exercises to strengthen our muscles and did some sports for fun when the P.E. teachers were busy doing something else. After I told him that, he was furious.

"How come they never taught you about your powers. That school was one of the best, it's not like them to do something like that. Wait…if she's behind this then it makes sense," John said.

"What do you mean by that," I replied.

"They must have purposely ignored your power training so that you wouldn't be able to resist when they take you away. For vampires, with or without training they would still be powerless. Demons are much powerful than any creature ever. The way their power works is connected to their emotions and thoughts. By putting the students, especially demons, in a peaceful environment for eight years must have left their powers in a coma. That way, it will be easier for them to kill you whenever they want. The reason behind them doing this is because of that lunatic woman. Her influence must have reached other schools. This situation is getting out of hand, we must prepare for our next move," John said.

His explanation does makes sense, but I still don't know how powerful this woman is. He would keep changing the topic if I asked him about her identity. It felt like were facing a wall. I couldn't imagine her doing all this alone, she must have had some ally helping her. I kept on wondering, how many children have she killed and tortured till now? My school didn't have many students, but more than half were killed. What about other schools, children outside the schools, children who don't have homes? What will happen to them? Was she doing this before?

I had so many questions I couldn't answer, and I don't think John is any help either. For now, one way of protecting children is by gaining my powers back. My powers will eventually come, but how long will I have to wait for them to come back? Is there any other way of getting them back faster?

"John, I can't continue living like this. If my power is connected to my emotion, wouldn't it be too dangerous if it suddenly came out. Don't you have any faster way to gain the powers back," I said.

"Hmmm…if that's the case, then I need to bring someone else for this job. I'm already busy with the house and considering my age, I don't think I can do well," John said.

"…so, you know someone who can help me?" I replied.

"Well…yes. She's not someone who can easily cooperate, but I'll try my luck. Keep in mind that I trust her more than anyone else. She's the same age as you, so I think you would get along well," John said being all smiley and weird.

I don't trust his words. For the first time he's praising someone other than himself. That seemed fishy to me. Thinking about it, having someone else in the house around my age seems fun. Everyone in this house is old, and I think I'm losing my young self when I'm with them. She must be special for John to ask her for help. Let's wait and see.

Blue Eyes

After waiting for a week, she's finally here arriving today. The person who is supposed to help me gain my power back. I don't know why I was excited like this, it's the first time I was acting like this. I was even waiting for her at the front door. I could hear John's giggling sound, but my eyes were focused on the door. Sitting on the floor without moving, waiting for the sound of the door opening. That was the most stressful moment in my life, even more stressful than being chased by a monster. It's all John's fault, he had been talking no stop about her and how amazing she is. Which is why I'm in this state right now.

Once the door opened, I immediately stood up. Being all excited just to see a stranger. Am I acting weird? Or is this normal reaction? Either way, she might be a nice person.

The butler came in first carrying so much luggage, while struggling to move forward. Then, she entered. Once she stepped inside, I stood there like a stone. I was mesmerized by her looks; she was so gorgeous. Tall, thin, short black hair, light blue eyes, white skin like snow, with big cherry lips. She's wearing black long-sleeved shirt, black pants, and long white coat. I think I found my dream girl.

She walked toward me and John being all confident. She greeted John first. Chatting and giggling with each other, I was standing there like a third wheel to a date. I could see Alfred standing far from us pitying me. Alfred, please stop.

She then turned to me and asked John about who I was. He told her that I am the prince he mentioned in the letter he wrote to her. I was surprised that he told her about my identity, so I confronted him about it. However, he said it was okay to tell her the truth since she's going to help us, and he seemed to trust her a lot.

"So? How do you know each other? And I still don't know your name," I asked the girl excitedly.

"Oh, I haven't greeted you yet. Hi, my name is Sofia. I'll be staying with you in this house from now on, helping you obtain your powers back as John mentioned in his letter. My job is anatomy, I'm focusing more on the anatomy of the demons and vampires. Since we, humans, must live with them, then there is bound to be mixed children. In order for us to heal them from diseases or injuries, we must first know about their internal organs, and how different are they from humans," she replied.

She also added, "As for how I met John, someone I knew introduced him to me. I came to this house when I was 11 years old and left two years ago. He helped me with my studies about anatomy, so I'm grateful to him." Then, she turned to John talking to him about something.

As she continues talking to John, I was staring at her not knowing where to look. Alfred came from behind saying, "She is indeed a beauty, but her personality isn't that good. You need to be careful not to mess with her." Well, he says that, but I don't think she's that bad. She can't be worse than

John, so I thought it will be alright. It's not like I like her or something, it's just that I've never met someone that is as beautiful as she is. In this house, I'm surrounded by demons and old men. For the school, the student there weren't really that good-looking, they were average. Am I being mean?

For a human, she is indeed a beauty.

I must've been staring for too long, because she suddenly turned to me and said, "What are you looking at, dumb face." I was shocked, it happened so suddenly. Alfred whispered with a smile on his face, "I told you so, her personality is not good."

"What? Am I not allowed to stare?" I replied.

"Come on, she didn't mean to say that, right Sofia?" John said while holding his laugh.

"I meant what I said. What are you going to do? Dumb face," she said.

"You…Who are you calling dumb face? Y-you b-blue eyes," I said furiously.

"Are you trying to curse me? You suck at that, you know," she said mockingly.

We kept on arguing, while John and Alfred standing there struggling to hold their laughter.

Please forget what I said before, her beauty disappeared once she opened her mouth. She was nice at first, I wonder what happened. She was not Sofia anymore, she turned into John. She is now John the second. From now on I'll call her John the second. No wait, that's too long, blue eyes is shorter. Why did she have to open her mouth, now I only see John's face with short black hair. Her beauty vanished, and now I can't stop imagining John's face on her head.

Oh god, why do you have to be so cruel to me? Before it was a duo, John and Alfred, now it became a trio once she arrived. Do I really have to spend the rest of my like with these three? Life is indeed hard. Someone, please save me from this misery.

During our argument, Alfred stepped in to stop me from continuing. John went to Sofia's side to calm her down. She's the one who started it, she's the one with the bad attitude. Why is he going to HER side, and calming HER down?

"Sofia, you just came from a long trip. You must be tired. The butler will show you your room, so just go to your room and rest," John said with a smile on his face.

Without saying anything, she glared at me and left with the butler. John then turned to me and said, "Don't you have manners? Remember to respect your guests. She came all the way here to help you after all, so be grateful."

"Why are you scolding me for something I didn't do? She's the one who started it. She insulted me first. Am I supposed to just laugh it off?" I replied furiously.

"Whatever, just don't cause any problem to her. And be nice, it was hard to convince her to come here," he said that before he leaves.

So he's defending her now. Even if she's here to help me, there's no reason for her to be rude to me. I don't think we will get along if she continues being rude. Respect should be earned. Ahhh…this is giving me a headache. I better rest well if I'm going to see her next day.

The Outside World

This morning, I woke up later than I usually do. My headache is gone, and I'm full of energy. I felt like this was going to be a beautiful and a happy day. I headed down for breakfast. I opened the door to the dining room, John and blue eyes were there. As I entered, they stood up and headed toward me being all smiley and disgusting.

"Why did you wake up late? We almost finished the food on the table. I'll ask Alfred to make something new for you, but it will take time. Make sure you wake up early next time, okay?" he said.

"John, let him wake up whenever he wants, I'm sure there will be leftovers for him somewhere," said John the second.

Right, this is John's house. There is no happy and beautiful day with them here.

I just walked past them without saying anything. I sat down and waited for Alfred to bring the food. They stood there silently, then just left without saying anything. John looked confused at first, but he just went along with it. I'm not letting her or anyone else ruin this day for me.

The clock is ticking, no one is coming to the room. I was sitting there alone, waiting for the food. It was relaxing, but I was starving. I can't function well without eating properly.

Alfred, please hurry. This day was supposed to be a happy day, there is no harm in waiting. Even with the food being late, I can still enjoy my time without John or anyone else ruining my mood.

After an hour, the door opened. I immediately turned my head checking who is entering the room. Sadly, it was blue eyes. I was disappointed. She was reading a book as she walked in. She raised her head and our eyes met. She smirked a little, and I looked away.

"Pfft…poor thing, did Alfred forget to bring you the food? You must be starving. If I were you, I would have yelled at him for being late," she said.

"Hmph…of course you would. Unlike you, I respect others. Don't you know that it takes time to prepare food? He must be busy with other things, that's why he is late. Also, I'm not that hungry. I can wait for him to come," I said.

After I said that, my stomach started making noises. Silence filled the room for a moment, then she started laughing hysterically. Why stomach, why did you have to embarrass me like that? Your timing is not good at all. I'll just pretend I didn't hear anything and stay quiet for a while. She kept on laughing and was barely able to stand. I looked away trying to hide my embarrassment, but I couldn't. She stood up while wiping her tears and said that she will go and call Alfred to bring the food then left the room.

Again, I was left alone in this room. I tried not to think about it, embarrassing things happens all the time. I tried to convince myself, but it was no use. The damage has already happened.

15 minutes later, Alfred entered the room with the food. As he approached me, I noticed that he was sweating, and he

looked exhausted. I asked him if he was okay, he replied saying he is fine and apologized for being late. Apparently, he prepared the food an hour ago and told another butler to bring it to me, but the other butler forgot to do so. When John the second told him about me waiting, he rushed to heat the food and walked as fast as he could to bring the food to me. He kept apologizing even though I told him it's fine. He then excused himself to return to his work. I started eating and thank God no one is here. If they saw me eating, they will be disgusted by the view. I mean, imagine being locked away for a long time and you see food for the first time, how do you think you would look like when you eat? No time for table manners.

I sat there after finishing the food, resting for a while. Alfred said to leave the plates here, but I felt bad seeing him exhausted. Before leaving I took the plates with me and headed to the kitchen. No one was there, so I just left them beside the sink and left.

I wandered around the house for a bit. No one was there. I headed to the library, opened the door and found John and blue eyes there. They were discussing about something. I approached them and asked about the butlers' whereabout.

"The butlers are rebuilding the storage outside. We are turning the storage to a lab where Sofia will use it to do researches about you. It's an old storage behind the mansion. No one will disturb you there," John said.

Then they continued with what they were talking about, so I left them alone. I wanted to go and see their work, but John prevented me from going outside the house. Every house has a roof, right? Maybe I can see them from the roof. I walked around searching for the stairs that lead to the roof. I found the stairs on the far corner, but I thought I might get hungry while watching them. I went downstairs to the kitchen and took some cookies and water with me, then headed back to the roof. I opened the door to the flat roof, went to the plain parapet wall where I could see them properly. I sat on the parapet wall placing the cookies and water on my left side. Is it weird to watch people work? I don't know, but I had nothing else to do. The weather was nice, it was neither hot nor it was cold. I could see them working hard. Alfred was standing there telling them what to do. All the butlers are vampires, I'm sure they will finish the work easily. Well…except for Alfred.

Time passed as I watched them from above. I heard the back-door opening, John stepped out and walked toward Alfred. They were talking but I couldn't hear them from above. Then, the roof door opened slowly making loud noises, it was an old rusty door. Blue eyes stepped in and walked towards me. I didn't want to talk to her, so I stayed quiet. She got closer, then sat next to me. Does she not know that sitting on the roof is dangerous? If she fell, I'm not catching her.

We sat there quietly, looking down. She then turned to me and kept staring. I tried to ignore her, but her stares were uncomfortable. So, I turned to her and said,

"What are you staring at? Am I too handsome that you can't look away?"

"Ha…you wish. I was waiting for you to notice my existence. It seems that you always ignore me."

"Ooohh…so you've noticed that I'm ignoring you, I didn't know you were THIS smart."

"Ughh…you're such a kid."

"So, why were you staring?"

"If you want to know that badly, then I guess I can tell you. I was analyzing your form. Your form is a mystery to me, everything about you is human. Well…except for your eyes and hair. I've met a lot of mixed children, but none of them had a full human body. I'm talking mainly about mixed demon kids. John didn't seem to know why either, so I'm just thinking about that."

"Well, this is how I looked ever since I was young. I don't think there is a reason for how I look."

"If you say so, your highness."

"Don't say that, it feels weird."

"Ha-ha…why, you're going to be the king someday. I'm just ensuring my safety."

"Being the king? I'm not sure about that."

"You don't want to?"

"No, I don't. John said before that I'm going to be the king, but I doubt it. I wasn't raised to be a king; I grew up like other normal kids. Besides, what do you think will happen if the world knew the prince is alive. Do you think they will kindly welcome you? Of course not. Even if it was revealed that I'm alive, I wouldn't accept the king position. I have zero knowledge on ruling a country."

"But how is the world able to function normally if the king and his son are not in the ruling position?"

"If the king died before appointing his successor, and he has no sons or relatives, then the nobility council will decide who will be the king. If they couldn't decide, then the council will take charge ruling the world. They mentioned something like that back in school."

"Hmmm…that seems complicated. So, what are you going to do in the future?"

"I'll decide when the time comes. For now, I just want my powers back."

"SOFIAA, COME DOWN!" John shouted.

"It seems they need me down there. Well, I should get going. Don't worry, I'll make sure you gain your powers back, that's why I'm here…then, see ya."

She turned around and left. In that moment, I had so many thoughts in my head. I was left wondering if it's okay to continue like this. All I did in this house was just sitting, eating, walking around and nothing else. No one asked me to do things for them. They don't worry about me. I was always alone in this house. Back in my parents' house, in school, in this mansion I'm being left alone from time to time. What's the point in doing anything, what's the point of living if I'm just going to sit around and do nothing for the rest of my life?

As I was wondering about so many things, the back door opened. John the second stepped out and walked towards John.

Ughh…look at them talking and smiling. Why is he so nice to her? What about me? Ever since I came to this house, I've never seen him smile like that to anyone, especially me. He accepted to teach her and took her in, while he refused to do the same thing to me and sent me to school. Not only John, even the butlers like her. What did I do to be treated like this?

I think I'm going crazy about this. Am I thinking too much about it? I think it's normal for others to treat girls differently. Sometimes I wonder if I'm going to continue to live with John in this house if I rejected on being the king.

This irritates me so much.

The Guest

Weeks have passed, and the construction of the lab was finally over. It's not like I did anything during that, I just sat on the roof watching them and sometimes went to the library when I got bored watching them. John was busy telling the butlers what to do. Alfred was guiding the rest of the butlers, and blue eyes was taking books from the library and going to her room. I'm sure she was researching about something.

I was alone during all that, as always. The demons were all sent outside for protection, that what John told me. I've tried cooking once, since everyone was busy, but I almost burned the kitchen. I was prohibited to step inside the kitchen after that. I mean, you have to explore your talents when you're all alone and have nothing to do, but I guess I don't have any.

Anyway, the work didn't stop there. After finishing the lab, they spent three days cleaning and furnishing the lab.

After finishing the lab, blue eyes announced that a guy she knows will come and stay in this house so they can work together. John didn't seem to mind letting strangers come and go as they please, but I do. I told him that we shouldn't trust anyone who comes, and it's too risky to let strangers in especially during these times where the enemy could attack anytime. That old man just shrugged his shoulders and left. Like the hell was that, am I the only sane one in this house? Well if he doesn't care, then why should I? It's not my house anyway.

Three days have passed, and the guest was on his way to John's house. Butlers were busy preparing dinner and cleaning around. I was standing near the stairs facing the front door waiting for him to enter, since no one is doing so. John and blue eyes were talking as they walked down the stairs. She was holding a glass of red wine in her right hand and was dressed nicely. As they reached me, blue eyes tripped on the last step of the stairs, and I was splashed by the red wine that she was holding.

"Is this intentional?"

"Wh-what? Of course not. I'm really sorry about that, I should have paid more attention. Just go take a shower first, Alfred will prepare more decent clothing for you."

"What do you mean decent? What's wrong with what I'm wearing?"

"Licht, that's enough. Go take a shower and change. We will be waiting here for our guest, come down when you finish."

There was no way that was unintentional. She must think I have a poor taste in clothing, these clothes were prepared by Alfred as well. Should I tell Alfred? It would be nice to see him get angry at her. As I was walking up the stairs, I looked down and she smiled and waved at me. Tha-that son of a- …that was definitely intentional. I see that you went low, but I can go even lower. Just wait, I'll show you how low I can go once I finish showering.

I went back to my room, and Alfred was there standing outside.

"I have prepared more decent clothing for you as she requested, young master. I was told to wait here for you, and take you back once you've finished."

Poor Alfred, I can feel his anger. I went inside, and the clothes that was prepared seemed a little…well how can I say it…flashy? They look terrible, there is no way I'm wearing this. This is bad, she really wanted to humiliate me in front of the guest. Whatever, I'll just take a shower and ask Alfred to help me put this thing on.

I finished my shower and wore pants and a shirt before putting on that hideous thing. I called Alfred several times, but he didn't reply, he usually comes inside whenever I call him. I opened the door looking for him in case he didn't hear me, but no one was there. I heard some noises behind me, it wasn't that loud. I turned my head slowly, and found Alfred lying there with a lot of blood on the floor and his body covered in wounds. I rushed to his side quickly, shaking and calling him, but he didn't move or say anything. I trembled in fear while looking around, he then suddenly grabbed my arm and kept repeating, "Run," in a shivering voice. I grabbed his hand trying to take him somewhere safe. Before I could stand up, I got hit in the head from behind. I lost my balance and fell on the floor. I tried to look behind, but all I could see before getting the second hit in the head was a purple high heel and a whip being held by the attacker. After that second hit, I lost my conscious.

Purple Lady

Instead of taking my time gaining my conscious back, I was splashed by water, which was effective I can't deny that. I mean how else are you supposed to wake someone up, by splashing them with water of course. Thanks to that, I regained my conscious. I opened my eye, and everything was spinning and foggy. I slowly started to see properly, and checked my surroundings. I was in a room with four cement walls, a wood chair on the right side, and a door far from me. My arms were chained up and my legs were tied together, I looked like a meat hanging and was ready to be cooked. A minute after gaining conscious, the door opened, and a lady walked in. She was wearing a purple sleeveless, long dress with crystals on it. She had a white fur scarf around her neck, wearing a purple high heel, purple lipstick, and holding a black whip in her right hand. She also had a long purple hair. She is a purple lady indeed.

"Oh, you're awake already?"

"Well, someone splashed me with water, so of course I would wake up."

"You were unconscious for a long time, so I thought this will help you wake up."

"So, you splashed me with water and just left? You could have waited for me to wake up."

"Why bother?"

She closed the door, and walked towards me.

"Nice whip you got there, what a delicate lady like you doing holding that thing?"

"Delicate? Me? Hahaha…you think sweet talk can get you out of here?"

"No harm in trying, am I right?"

"Well, since you like it, why don't I show you how it's used?"

She then proceeded to hit me with it. She hit me five times on my chest, then went behind me and hit me five times on my back.

"Ha…so…do you…ha…still think I'm delicate now?"

"Well you are, seeing that you can barely breathe after hitting someone with a whip. You can rest for a while, I'm not going anywhere."

"At least show that you're in pain. I can't believe you can talk normally after that."

"Well, people call me emotionless. I guess they were right."

She grabbed the wood chair, dragged it, and placed it in front of me. She sat on the chair, and took a deep breath. I waited for her to calm down, blood was dripping down. The wounds I got from the whip hurt a lot, if I showed her pain then she might get excited and continue. She locked me here in this miserable place, there is no telling how crazy she is.

"Why are you doing this?"

"Well, it all started when I got married to a vampire. The world was against our marriage, and because of tha—"

"Stop, I don't care about your past. You're not going to make a speech about how you became the villain, are you?"

"You asked why I'm doing this."

"Yeah, if you're going to tell me your entire past then I don't care. Just do what you want. Nobody got time for that."

"You…I should have killed when I had the chance to."

"But you didn't."

"It's all because of her. She wanted you alive."

"Her? You're working with someone?"

"Why should I tell you? You're going to see her anyway, she is coming here soon."

It seems that she's dumber than I thought. Getting information from her might be easy. She might get suspicious if I asked her many questions, I better stay quiet for now.

Few minutes later, someone knocked three times on the door. The purple lady got up excitedly and rushed to the door while shouting, "She's here." She opened the door and invited the girl inside. The girt was wearing a black hooded cape covering her head. She walked behind the purple lady toward me. She removed the hood from her head and revealed herself.

"Sofia?"

"What? you two know each other?"

"A little."

"What are you doing here? What happened to John?"

"I'll tell you later."

"Pfffff…you got betrayed, that's what happened. I've already sent my men after the rest of the survivors. It won't be long till they find them and finish every one of them."

"Sofia, say something."

"Hahahaha…look at you. You didn't show any emotion when I hit you with the whip, but now you're worried about the old man. You are really something else."

This lunatic woman kept laughing at my miserable state. I got furious, if I had my powers, I would have chopped her head off. Blood kept dripping on the floor as I tried to free myself. Sofia took out a dagger and stabbed her from behind. The purple lady's smile slowly faded as she fell to the ground. Sofia took out the dagger and stabbed her leg out of nowhere. She then screamed, "HELP," as loud as she could. Few butlers rushed inside, one carried her out, another took the purple lady, and the rest freed me. Once my feet touched the floor, I got dizzy and fell to the ground.

The End?

I woke up after the incident in my room lying on my bed, bandages all over my body and head. The door opened, Sofia and John entered the room. I felt the pain as I tried to sit.

"What happened?"

"What happened is we got attacked by that lunatic woman while we were waiting for the guests to come. Luckily, we were able to hide in the safe room. One of the butlers told us that they took you away and left the house. So, I sent a group of butlers to search for you. The demons I sent out for protection were killed somehow."

"Safe room? I didn't know there was a safe room. What about Alfred? Is Alfred okay? He was bleeding before I was taken away."

"Unfortunately, he died. We couldn't do anything."

"And that crazy woman?"

"She's dead. It was good that Sofia found you."

"Found me? She was working with that crazy lady."

"What are you talking about? She's not working with anyone. You got hit in the head and now you're imagining things."

"What? I know what I saw. She was the—"

"John, it's best to let me handle him. He's been through a lot."

John looked at me and agreed with her then left. I'm not crazy, she was definitely there. I knew what I saw. Was she lying to him? Should I confront her? Since John trust her a lot, it would be hard for me to convince him.

"Too much talking is not good for you. You've been sleeping for three days, make sure to rest if you want your wounds to heal."

"Why are you lying to him?"

"He doesn't have to know all the details, does he? Let me cut the apple for you. You must be hungry."

She was smiling and humming as she peeled the apple. She didn't seem to want to talk about it. Well, whatever she does is not my business anyway. I was saved by her after all, but I don't think I can trust her from now on. She must be up to something. Alfred is dead now; John is all I have left. I can't let her hurt him. I don't know what she is capable of, so it's better to not provoke her.

"By the way, who was that woman?"

"You don't know? Didn't you listen to her speech about why she did that?"

"Yeah, no. I wasn't interested in her past, so I just stopped her. She didn't tell me after."

"Wow, I'm surprised she didn't kill you after you stopped her."

"So, who is she?"

"Haa...she is the one who killed those mixed kids. Well...she ordered her servant to kill them, she didn't do it directly."

"What? She didn't seem capable of doing that."

"Hmmm…I didn't know you were this smart. It might be hard to believe, but it's true. However, it doesn't mean she was working alone. She must've had few powerful partners."

"Ha…how could someone this crazy gain support?"

"She uses her body."

"What?"

"Enough talking. You should eat some apples and rest."

She then shoved one of the apple pieces into my mouth. I almost choked on the apple. Damn it, I might die someday because of her.

After two weeks of resting and being in my room all the time, I could finally walk around the house. I headed down for dinner. The house was empty, I didn't see anyone as I headed down. It might be because they were busy, since a lot of butlers were killed. Anyway, I won't let what happened ruin my happiness for today. I reached the dining room, opened the door and were shocked to see everyone there glaring at me. I don't remember annoying someone, so why the glares.

"Wh-why are you glaring at me? I swear I didn't do anything."

"Butlers, throw him outside."

"Wait, what? Hey."

The butlers came closer, dragged me to the front door, and threw me outside the house.

"What are you doing?"

"Traitors like you have no place in my house."

"Traitor? When did I ever betray you? I haven't done anything."

"Done nothing wrong? Then, why are you refusing to be the king? I'm doing my best to make you the king, so why are you refusing it? Were you trying to deceive me so that you can live in this house as you want? If it wasn't for Sofia telling me, I would have stayed being deceived by you."

"John, stop. Don't do this to him."

"Sofia, don't defend him."

"So what? You're calling me a traitor just for refusing to be the king? Weren't you the one who decided to help me after my parents' death, claiming that you're my dad's friend?"

"I only took you in because I thought you're going to be the king someday. Otherwise, no would want someone like you."

"Wha—"

"John, stop. If you kick him out, then what about me? What about the lab? I only came here to help him gain his power back, and build the lab to do experiments."

"Does he even have powers? Forget about this imbecile, you can live here if you want, the lab is all yours."

He said that and went inside with his butlers and closed the door. Sofia stayed outside while I was on my knees, shocked. She turned to me and smiled. Are you pitying me? Stop looking at me with those eyes.

"This is all your fault. If you stayed quiet, none of this would have happened."

"After seeing how he reacted, now you're blaming me? You should be thankful that I exposed him to you."

"The hell are you talking about."

"Let me say this, and make sure you remember it clearly until you die."

She moved closer and whispered in my ears.

"I'm the only one you can trust in this world. I'll always believe you, more than anyone. I'll crush everyone who tries to hurt you, no matter who they are."

She moved away, patted on my head with a gentle smile, and left. She opened the door, smiled gently and waved, then went inside.

I had no idea of what's going on anymore. Alfred is dead, John is going insane, and Sofia is…what am I supposed to do now? How am I supposed to survive in this world? My life turned upside down in a second, just for refusing to be the king. No wonder John didn't care about me as much as he does to Sofia. I'm nothing to him, just a toy that will take him to the top.

Haha…this must be a joke. Kick me out, don't make me laugh. Who needs you anyway, I can survive on my own. Just sit there and watch me live my life, you ugly old man. I'll do everything to survive, even if I had to be the villain. No one will be able to stop me.

And now it started raining. Why? I'm not sad. Rain only happens when the main character is sad. That's what happens in every story I've read. Whatever, I'll just find some place to hide from the rain.

For everyone in this house, I will return someday for my revenge. No one will be safe from me when that happens, just wait and see.

CPSIA information can be obtained
at www.ICGtesting.com
Printed in the USA
LVHW080448010622
720088LV00009B/819